FLOWER FAIRIES
THE
LITTLE PINK BOOK

FLOWER FAIRIES
THE
LITTLE PINK BOOK

CICELY MARY BARKER
FREDERICK WARNE

FREDERICK WARNE

Penguin Books Ltd, Harmondsworth, Middlesex, England
New York, Australia, Canada, New Zealand

First Published 1994
1 3 5 7 9 10 8 6 4 2

ISBN 0 7232 0025 4

Printed and bound by
Tien Wah Press, Singapore

CONTENTS

The Candytuft Fairy

The Phlox Fairy

The Sweet Pea Fairies

The Daisy Fairy

The Larch Fairy

The Herb Robert Fairy

The Foxglove Fairy

The Wild Rose Fairy

The Honeysuckle Fairy

The Heather Fairy

The Rose Fairy

The Spindle Berry Fairy

A

Apple Blossom

Columbine

Fuchsia

◆ THE SONG OF ◆
THE FUCHSIA FAIRY

Fuchsia is a dancer
Dancing on her toes,
Clad in red and purple,
By a cottage wall;
Sometimes in a greenhouse,
In frilly white and rose,
Dressed in her best for the fairies' evening ball!

(This is the little out-door Fuchsia.)

◆ THE SONG OF ◆
THE JASMINE FAIRY

In heat of summer days
With sunshine all ablaze,
Here, here are cool green bowers,
Starry with Jasmine flowers;
Sweet-scented, like a dream
Of Fairyland they seem.

And when the long hot day
At length has worn away,
And twilight deepens, till
The darkness comes—then, still,
The glimmering Jasmine white
Gives fragrance to the night.

J

Jasmine

Mallow

◆ THE SONG OF ◆
THE MALLOW FAIRY

I am Mallow; here sit I
Watching all the passers-by.
Though my leaves are torn and tattered,
Dust-besprinkled, mud-bespattered,
See, my seeds are fairy cheeses,
Freshest, finest, fairy cheeses!
These are what an elf will munch
For his supper or his lunch.
Fairy housewives, going down
To their busy market-town,
Hear me wheedling: "Lady, please,
Pretty lady, buy a cheese!"
And I never find it matters
That I'm nicknamed Rags-and-Tatters,
For they buy my fairy cheeses,
Freshest, finest, fairy cheeses!

◆ THE SONG OF ◆
THE ORCHIS FAIRY

The families of orchids,
　　they are the strangest clan,
With spots and twists resembling
　　a bee, or fly, or man;
And some are in the hot-house,
　　and some in foreign lands,
But Early Purple Orchis
　　in English pasture stands.

He loves the grassy hill-top,
　　he breathes the April air;
He knows the baby rabbits,
　　he knows the Easter hare,
The nesting of the skylarks,
　　the bleat of lambkins too,
The cowslips, and the rainbow,
　　the sunshine, and the dew.

O orchids of the hot-house,
　　what miles away you are!
O flaming tropic orchids,
　　how far, how very far!

Orchis

R

Ragged   Robin

◆ THE SONG OF ◆
THE RAGGED ROBIN FAIRY

In wet marshy meadows
A tattered piper strays——
Ragged, ragged Robin;
On thin reeds he plays.

He asks for no payment;
He plays, for delight,
A tune for the fairies
To dance to, at night.

They nod and they whisper,
And say, looking wise,
"A princeling is Robin,
For all his disguise!"

◆ THE SONG OF ◆
THE THRIFT FAIRY

Now will we tell of splendid things:
Seagulls, that sail on fearless wings
Where great cliffs tower, grand and high
Against the blue, blue summer sky.
Where none but birds (and sprites) can go.
Oh there the rosy sea-pinks grow,
(Sea-pinks, whose other name is Thrift);
They fill each crevice, chink, and rift
Where no one climbs; and at the top,
Too near the edge for sheep to crop,
Thick in the grass pink patches show.
The sea lies sparkling far below.
Oh lucky Thrift, to live so free
Between blue sky and bluer sea!

T

Thrift

Zinnia

• THE SONG OF •
THE ZINNIA FAIRY

Z for Zinnias, pink or red;
See them in the flower-bed,
Copper, orange, all aglow,
Making such a stately show.

I, their fairy, say Good-bye,
For the last of all am I.
Now the Alphabet is said
All the way from A to Z.

• THE SONG OF •
THE FUMITORY FAIRY

Given me hundreds of years ago,
My name has a meaning you shall know:
It means, in the speech of the bygone folk,
"Smoke of the Earth" —a soft green smoke!

A wonderful plant to them I seemed;
Strange indeed were the dreams they dreamed,
Partly fancy and partly true,
About "Fumiter" and the way it grew.

Where men have ploughed
    or have dug the ground,
Still, with my rosy flowers, I'm found;
Known and prized by the bygone folk
As "Smoke of the Earth" —
    a soft green smoke!

(The name "Fumitory" was "Fumiter" 300 years ago;
and long before that, "Fume Terre", which is the French
name, still, for the plant. "Fume means "smoke", "terre"
means "earth".)

The Fumitory Fairy

The Stork's-Bill Fairy

◆ THE SONG OF ◆
THE STORK'S-BILL FAIRY

"Good morning, Mr Grasshopper!
  Please stay and talk a bit!"
"Why yes, you pretty Fairy;
  Upon this grass I'll sit.
And let us ask some riddles;
  They're better fun than chat:
Why am I like the Stork's-bill?
  Come, can you answer *that?*"

"Oh no, you clever Grasshopper!
  I fear I am a dunce;
I cannot guess the answer—
  I give it up at once!"
"When children think they've caught me,
  I'm gone, with leap and hop;
And when they gather Stork's—bill,
  Why, all the petals drop!"

(The Stork's-bill gets her name from the long seed-pod,
which looks like a stork's beak or bill. Others of her family
are called Crane's-bills.)

◆ THE SONG OF ◆
THE PINK FAIRIES

Early in the mornings,
   when children still are sleeping,
Or late, late at night-time,
   beneath the summer moon,
What are they doing,
   the busy fairy people?
Could you creep to spy them,
   in silent magic shoon,

You might learn a secret,
   among the garden borders,
Something never guessed at,
   that no one knows or thinks:
Snip, snip, snip, go busy fairy scissors,
Pinking out the edges
   of the petals of the Pinks!

Pink Pinks, white Pinks,
   double Pinks, and single,——
Look at them and see
   if it's not the truth I tell!
Why call them Pinks
   if they weren't pinked out by *someone*?
And what but fairy scissors
   could pink them out so well?

The Pink Fairies

The Candytuft Fairy

✦ THE SONG OF ✦
THE CANDYTUFT FAIRY

Why am I "Candytuft"?
That I don't know!
Maybe the fairies
First called me so;
Maybe the children,
Just for a joke;
(I'm in the gardens
Of most little folk).

Look at my clusters!
See how they grow:
Some pink or purple,
Some white as snow;
Petals uneven,
Big ones and small;
Not very tufty—
No candy at all!

◆ THE SONG OF ◆
THE PHLOX FAIRY

August in the garden!
Now the cheerful Phlox
Makes one think of country-girls
Fresh in summer frocks.

There you see magenta,
Here is lovely white,
Mauve, and pink, and cherry-red—
Such a pleasant sight!

Smiling little fairy
Climbing up the stem,
Tell us which is prettiest?
She says, "All of them!"

The Phlox Fairy

The Sweet Pea Fairies

◆ THE SONG OF ◆
THE SWEET PEA FAIRIES

Here Sweet Peas are climbing;
  (Here's the Sweet Pea rhyme!)
Here are little tendrils,
  Helping them to climb.

Here are sweetest colours;
  Fragrance very sweet;
Here are silky pods of peas,
  Not for us to eat!

Here's a fairy sister,
  Trying on with care
Such a grand new bonnet
  For the baby there.

Does it suit you, Baby?
  Yes, I really think
Nothing's more becoming
  Than this pretty pink!

◆ THE SONG OF ◆
THE DAISY FAIRY

Come to me and play with me,
　　I'm the babies' flower;
Make a necklace gay with me,
Spend the whole long day with me,
　　Till the sunset hour.

I must say Good-night, you know,
　　Till tomorrow's playtime;
Close my petals tight, you know,
Shut the red and white, you know,
　　Sleeping till the daytime.

The Daisy Fairy

The Larch
Fairy

The Larch Fairy

◆ THE SONG OF ◆
THE LARCH FAIRY

Sing a song of Larch trees
　　Loved by fairy-folk;
Dark stands the pinewood,
　　Bare stands the oak,
But the Larch is dressed and trimmed
　　Fit for fairy-folk!

Sing a song of Larch trees,
　　Sprays that swing aloft,
Pink tufts, and tassels
　　Grass-green and soft:
All to please the little elves
　　Singing songs aloft!

◆ THE SONG OF ◆
THE HERB ROBERT FAIRY

Little Herb Robert,
 Bright and small,
Peeps from the bank
 Or the old stone wall.

Little Herb Robert,
 His leaf turns red;
He's wild geranium,
 So it is said.

The Herb Robert Fairy

The Foxglove Fairy

◆ THE SONG OF ◆
THE FOXGLOVE FAIRY

"Foxglove, Foxglove,
   What do you see?"
The cool green woodland,
   The fat velvet bee;
Hey, Mr Bumble,
   I've honey here for thee!

"Foxglove, Foxglove,
   What see you now?"
The soft summer moonlight
   On bracken, grass, and bough;
And all the fairies dancing
   As only they know how.

• THE SONG OF •
THE WILD ROSE FAIRY

I am the queen whom everybody knows:
    I am the English Rose;
As light and free as any Jenny Wren,
    As dear to Englishmen;
As joyous as a Robin Redbreast's tune,
    I scent the air of June;
My buds are rosy as a baby's cheek;
    I have one word to speak,
One word which is my secret and my song,
'Tis "England, England, England" all day long.

The Wild Rose Fairy

The Honeysuckle Fairy

◆ THE SONG OF ◆
THE HONEYSUCKLE FAIRY

The lane is deep, the bank is steep,
  The tangled hedge is high;
And clinging, twisting, up I creep,
  And climb towards the sky.
O Honeysuckle, mounting high!
O Woodbine, climbing to the sky!

The people in the lane below
  Look up and see me there,
Where I my honey-trumpets blow,
  Whose sweetness fills the air.
O Honeysuckle, waving there!
O Woodbine, scenting all the air!

♦ THE SONG OF ♦
THE HEATHER FAIRY

"Ho, Heather, ho! From south to north
Spread now your royal purple forth!
Ho, jolly one! From east to west,
The moorland waiteth to be dressed!"

I come, I come! With footsteps sure
I run to clothe the waiting moor;
From heath to heath I leap and stride
To fling my bounty far and wide.

(The heather in the picture is bell heather, or heath; it is
different from the common heather which is also called ling.)

The Heather Fairy

◆ THE SONG OF ◆
THE ROSE FAIRY

Best and dearest flower that grows,
Perfect both to see and smell;
Words can never, never tell
Half the beauty of a Rose—
Buds that open to disclose
Fold on fold of purest white,
Lovely pink, or red that glows
Deep, sweet-scented. What delight
    To be Fairy of the Rose!

The Rose Fairy

◆ THE SONG OF ◆
THE SPINDLE BERRY FAIRY

See the rosy-berried Spindle
All to sunset colours turning,
Till the thicket seems to kindle,
Just as though the trees were burning.
While my berries split and show
Orange-coloured seeds aglow,
One by one my leaves must fall:
Soon the wind will take them all.
Soon must fairies shut their eyes
For the Winter's hushabies;
But, before the Autumn goes,
Spindle turns to flame and rose!